Lulu and Lainey

... a French Yarn

For every child who has lost a favorite object. May it always find its way back home…

ISBN-13: 978-1518681851
ISBN-10: 1518681859

Lulu loved to knit.

She especially loved to knit with her Grand-mère.

They spent many happy hours together making hats and scarves to keep warm against the winds coming across the River Seine during cold Paris winters.

But this was a Saturday in springtime. The weather was beautiful with the lovely fragrance of flowers and fresh-baked bread on warm breezes.

The trees were in bloom ~ sometimes sending little
petals floating down, which looked like colorful snow
on the ground.

Lulu was happy as she walked through the park to Grand-mère's apartment.

She had her favorite ball of fuzzy green yarn with her. She called the yarn "Lainey", like the French word for wool.

She planned to use it to make a special scarf with Grand-mère.

Lulu saw her friends, Pierre and Noémi, playing soccer in the park.

"Lulu, come play with us," they called.

She dropped her knitting basket under a tree. "Just for a few minutes - I'm going to knit with my Grand-mère," she called as she ran to kick the soccer ball.

Soon Lulu realized she was going to be late.

She grabbed the handle of her knitting basket and ran off.

When she arrived at Grand-mère's apartment Lulu saw that her favorite yarn was not in her knitting basket. "I must go back to the park," she said with tears in her eyes.

Lulu ran back to the park and looked under the tree, but Lainey was not there.

Lulu returned to Grand-mère's apartment and sadly shared the unhappy news. She wondered if she would ever see the ball of yarn again.

Grand-mère comforted her while they drank strawberry tea and ate biscuits.

Here's what happened.

When Lulu ran off with her knitting basket, Lainey fell out and rolled under a bush.

A mother bird looking for worms hopped by and saw Lainey.

She had two eggs in her nest in the tree, but Lainey looked like another egg to her.

She got hold of Lainey and carried her up into the tree.

Lainey dropped into the nest where two beautiful green eggs were resting.

The mother bird sat on all of them, keeping them warm and cozy.

Then, one day…

… there were sounds coming from inside the eggs, like tapping on a door. Before she knew it, a baby bird hatched out of each egg.

The baby birds grew and grew. When the mother bird flew off to find food, they would huddle close to Lainey for warmth.

Spring turned into summer and as the days began to shorten, the mother bird knew it was time to teach her babies to fly.

One morning both baby birds flew off, knocking
Lainey out of the nest and

down,

down,

down.

Lainey landed under the tree – right into Lulu's knitting basket!

The birds flew around, waving a fond farewell to their fuzzy friend.

Lulu was once again in the park playing soccer with friends on her way to Grand-mère's house.

And once again her knitting basket was under the tree.

When Lulu came back to get the basket, she saw
Lainey and let out a great cheer.

"Lainey, where have you been? How did you get into my basket? Did you have an adventure? Where did those feathers come from?"

And, indeed, there were fluffy feathers sticking out of the strands of yarn, just like a little bonnet.

Lulu continued to Grand-mère's house with Lainey safe in her knitting basket.

They had a wonderful time knitting, while trying to guess where Lainey had been all this time.

Made in the USA
San Bernardino, CA
25 November 2016